JASON STRANGE

THE GRAVEYARD PLOT

Cover art by Alberto Dal Lago

Interior art by Nelson Evergreen

STONE ARCH
a capstone imprint

Jason Strange is published by Stone Arch Books
A Capstone Imprint
1710 Roe Crest Dr.
North Mankato, Minnesota 56003
www.capstonepub.com

Copyright © 2012 by Stone Arch Books

Cataloging-in-Publication Data is available at the Library of Congress website.

ISBN: 978-1-4342-3298-4 (library binding)
ISBN: 978-1-4342-3886-3 (paperback)

Summary: As Damon helps pack up his sickly grandfather's belongings, he stumbles upon
a strange map that leads directly to a nearby graveyard . . .

Art Director: Kay Fraser
Graphic Designer: Hilary Wacholz
Production Specialist: Michelle Biedscheid

Photo credits:
Shutterstock: Nikita Rogul (handcuffs, p. 2); Stephen Mulcahey (police badge, p. 2);
B&T Media Group (blank badge, p. 2); Picsfive (coffee stain, pp. 2, 5, 12, 17, 24, 30,
42, 48, 57); Andy Dean Photography (paper, pen, coffee, pp. 2, 66); osov (blank notes,
p. 1); Thomas M Perkins (folder with blank paper, pp. 66, 67); M.E. Mulder (black
electrical tape, pp. 69, 70, 71)

Printed in the United States of America in Stevens Point, Wisconsin.
102011   006404WZS12

TABLE OF CONTENTS

Chapter 1: Grandpa's Attic

Damon Germain stood on the front lawn of his grandfather's very old house. It was a huge building right on the edge of Ravens Pass. He'd been there many times before, but today was different. Today Grandpa wouldn't be there.

Standing next to Damon on the lawn were his mother; her friend, Martha Kane; and Martha's son, Jaden. The four of them lived in Lakeville, but they were all in Ravens Pass for the weekend just to pack up the house and prepare it to be put on the market.

Damon hardly knew Jaden, despite the fact that they were in the same grade at school. The only thing he did know about him was that Jaden had a reputation as a troublemaker. Jaden was only there because his mother didn't like the idea of leaving Jaden home alone. All the same, the Germains were glad to have some help packing and cleaning.

Martha shook her head. "It's such a shame," she said. "This house has been in your family since it was built almost a century ago!"

"I know," Damon's mother said. "But my dad just can't afford to keep the place anymore."

The four of them walked to the front porch. As they stepped inside the house, they saw that the place was a complete mess.

Jaden put a hand over his mouth and nose. "Wow, it kind of —" he started to say.

"Stinks," Damon's mother said. "I know." She sighed sadly. Then she nodded. "This is probably for the best. Dad will be happier and healthier at the home."

Martha put her hands on her hips and smiled. "We should break into teams," she said. "The moms will start in the basement."

"Great idea," Damon's mother said. "Damon and Jaden, you two head up to the attic and start packing up some of Grandpa's old junk. He's got a lot of it up there."

"Okay," Damon said. "Come on, Jaden. Let's get some boxes and get started."

Jaden grunted. "Whatever," he said.

The attic was practically a full third floor. It had a sloped ceiling that was very high in the middle but came right down to the floor on both sides. Along the walls were boxes and trunks, old furniture and lamps, and countless stacks of books. Everything was covered in a thick layer of dust.

"I don't think anybody's been up here in years," Damon said quietly.

"Gee, you think?" Jaden said. He ran a finger along the top of a desk. It left a trail in the dust. "This place is a dump."

"Right," Damon said, his smile drooping to a frown. "And we have to pack it all up."

"Great," Jaden said. He plopped down on a small antique couch. A spring creaked and a cloud of dust puffed up around him. He coughed and jumped off the couch.

"This is stupid," Jaden said. "Packing everything in here will take the whole weekend!"

Damon nodded. "If not longer," he said.

Jaden shook his head. "Not gonna happen," he said. "I've got better things to do."

Damon rolled his eyes. He unfolded one of the cardboard boxes so it was ready to be loaded up with stuff. "Then you'd better work fast," he said. "Because your mom said she wasn't leaving until everything's finished."

Jaden sighed. "I don't see why I'm even here," he said. "He's not my grandpa."

"Then don't help," Damon said, irritated. "It doesn't matter to me."

"Oh, relax," Jaden said. "I'll help."

"Good," Damon said. "Start over there."

Jaden walked over to an old trunk under a tiny window. He popped open the trunk. "What's in here?" he asked.

Damon ignored him and started packing various items into the box he'd opened. "We need newspaper or something," he muttered, looking at the vase he held in his hands. "This stuff is fragile."

"Weird," Jaden said. He pulled out a black-and-white photo and held it out toward Damon. "This kid looks just like you."

"Jaden," Damon said, "we're supposed to be packing — not unpacking! Just leave the trunk alone. It'll go into the truck as-is."

Jaden rolled his eyes. He held the photo closer to Damon's face. "Just look at this kid," he said. "He could be your twin!"

Damon scowled. He snatched the photo from Jaden and looked at it quickly. It was his grandpa. Next to him was a boy about the same age, but Damon didn't recognize him.

Damon handed the picture back to Jaden. "It's my grandpa," he said. "Looks like he was my age then. I don't recognize the other boy."

"Not your grandpa's brother?" Jaden asked.

Damon shook his head. "He didn't have one," he said. Damon got up and went back to the box he'd been packing. "Let's just get this over with," he said.

"I wonder who he is," Jaden said.

Damon shrugged. "If you're so curious," he said, "just keep the photo for now and ask my grandpa about it during lunch."

"Good idea," Jaden said. He shoved the photo into the back pocket of his jeans.

- Chapter 2: Grandpa -

The morning was filled with lifting, sorting, and dust. By early afternoon, Jaden and Damon were starving.

Mom's voice called out from downstairs. "You kids getting hungry yet?"

Damon and Jaden dropped what they were doing and sprinted down the big staircase. They met their mothers at the landing and slid to a stop, almost crashing into them.

"I guess that's a yes," Mom said, laughing.

Jaden and Damon nodded. "We're almost done packing up everything in the attic, Mom," Damon said.

"Already? I'm impressed!" his mother said, smiling. "Let's take a break and head over to the nursing home to have lunch with your grandpa."

* * *

Grandpa's new place was downtown at the Ravens Pass Assisted Living Home. It was a tall, red-brick building that had lots of windows. The grounds were green and surrounded by tall maple trees.

Damon's grandpa was in the lobby when they arrived. He was a little old man with a hunchback and a kind face. When he stood up, he wasn't much taller than Damon.

"Grandpa!" Damon said. He ran over and gave him a hug.

"Hello there, Damon," Grandpa said. "My goodness, you're growing fast! Pretty soon you'll be taller than me!"

"Hi, Dad," Damon's mother said. "You remember my friend, Martha Kane? This is her son, Jaden."

Grandpa smiled strangely at Jaden. "Nice to meet you, young man," he said.

Jaden pulled the photograph from his back pocket and held it out. "Who is this?" he asked. "He looks exactly like Damon."

Grandpa squinted at Jaden. He gently took the picture from him. Slowly, he pulled his reading glasses from the chest pocket of his shirt and carefully slipped them on. He focused his eyes on the photograph.

Grandpa's smile slipped away. For a few moments, he looked very sad.

"Are you all right, Dad?" Damon's mom asked.

Grandpa nodded. "I haven't seen this picture in many years," he said. "This boy was my friend when I was young."

Grandpa looked at Damon. "We were about your age in this picture," he said. Then Grandpa looked at Jaden. "And I would guess that Aaron was about your age, Jaden."

"His name was Aaron?" Jaden asked.

Grandpa tapped his nose. "Exactly," he said. "I remember the day this photo was taken very well."

"Dad, that photo was taken almost seventy years ago!" Ms. Germain said. "I doubt you remember what you did last week."

Grandpa pulled off his glasses and shot Damon's mom an annoyed smile. Then he turned back toward Jaden and handed the photo to him. "It was a day I'll never forget," Grandpa said. "Aaron disappeared that day, and I never saw him again."

Chapter 3: Curiosity

Damon, Jaden, their mothers, and Grandpa ate lunch together in the nursing home's dining hall. Lunch was Moroccan stew with flatbread and peas. Damon had three servings.

Grandpa spent most of the meal picking at his stew with a faraway look on his face. When Martha and Damon's mom got up to clear the table, Grandpa put down his fork and held out his hand toward Jaden.

"Give me that photo for a second," he said to Jaden. Jaden pulled the photo out from his pocket and handed it to Grandpa. With one bony finger, Grandpa pointed at something in the photo. "See that scrap of paper Aaron is holding?"

Jaden looked at the photo and nodded. "What is it?" he asked.

"That's the reason I never saw Aaron again," Grandpa said. "We thought we would just have some fun. And it was fun — for a while."

"What was fun, Grandpa?" Damon asked. "What is the paper?"

"That, Damon," Grandpa said, "is a treasure map."

Damon's jaw dropped. Jaden leaned forward. "A real treasure map?" Jaden asked.

Grandpa scowled. He gave Jaden a long stare. As Martha and Damon's mom sat down at the table again, Grandpa raised one long bent finger. He pointed at Jaden.

"I know that look," Grandpa said, like he was accusing Jaden of something.

Jaden leaned back. He opened his mouth, but no words came out. He trembled.

"That look is greed," Grandpa said. His finger began to shake. "I saw that look once before. And now Aaron is gone."

Suddenly Grandpa spun in his chair and faced Damon. His eyes were wild and muscles were tensed. "Don't let that boy take you on a treasure hunt, Damon!" he said. "You hear me?!"

"Dad, please," Damon's mom said quietly. "Calm down."

Grandpa ignored her. He stood up and took Jaden by the wrist. "It was the demon," he said. "The demon killed Aaron!"

An orderly wearing a white uniform got up from his seat in the corner. He quickly moved for their table.

"Don't go after that treasure!" Grandpa cried out. The orderly took him by the arm. "If you go after that treasure, someone will die!"

The orderly gently pulled Grandpa out of the dining hall. Another orderly walked up to the table. "Don't let it upset you," he said with a smile. "The first few days here are always hard, but folks adjust." He glanced down at Damon. "Your grandpa will be just fine, I promise."

The orderly turned to Damon's mom, and added, "You should let your father get some rest for now."

* * *

"I wish you two hadn't showed him that picture," Damon's mom said when they got into the car.

"We didn't mean to upset him," Damon said.

Martha patted Ms. Germain's hand. "You heard the orderly," she said. "Adjusting to a new home at that age must be difficult. I'm sure he's just stressed."

Damon's mom sighed. "You're right," she said. "It's not your fault, Damon. Or yours, Jaden."

Damon looked out the window as the car drove down the long driveway. "I didn't know he had a friend who went missing," he said.

"I didn't either," his mother said. "It's funny that he's never mentioned him before. He was obviously very important to him."

"Yeah," Jaden said. "And the treasure was obviously important to his friend, Aaron."

Damon glanced at Jaden. A wide smirk ran across Jaden's face.

Chapter 4: Troublemaker

Once they were on the road back to Grandpa's old house, Jaden leaned across the back seat toward Damon. Jaden's eyes seemed to light up.

"So?" Jaden whispered. "What do you think about that treasure map?"

"What about it?" Damon asked quietly.

"We should find it," Jaden said. He flashed Damon a wicked grin.

"Are you kidding me?" Damon said. "You heard Grandpa. Besides, who knows if the treasure map is even around anymore, not to mention the treasure itself. If either ever even existed."

Jaden kept smiling. "Don't be such a baby," he said. "There's nothing to be afraid of. You heard the orderly. Your grandpa's probably just getting senile."

Damon didn't answer. He just stared out the window.

"Besides," Jaden said, his voice softer now, "if we can find that treasure, I bet there would be enough money so that your grandpa wouldn't have to sell his house."

Damon hesitated. "I suppose it couldn't hurt to look," he said. "Maybe Grandpa kept the map in the same trunk where you found that photo."

Jaden nodded. "Probably," he said.

Damon asked, "But aren't you scared?"

Jaden nearly laughed. "Of course not," he said. "I'm not some little kid."

Damon turned away. He looked out the window at the tall, crooked elms that lined the street. "Neither am I," he said.

* * *

Cleaning in the afternoon was more difficult than the morning had been. Grandpa's bedroom wasn't that messy, but the other two bedrooms were filthy and filled with random items. Damon wondered if Grandpa had ever thrown anything away in the seventy-two years he'd lived there.

While they worked, Jaden kept bringing up the treasure map. "So?" he said. "Can we go look for it now?"

"I wish you'd just forget about it," Damon said. He unfolded another cardboard box. "We have a lot of work to do. There's no time to go on some silly treasure hunt."

"Oh, please," Jaden said. "We've got this thing in the bag! I checked with my mom, and they're almost done with the main floor already. They'll come up soon to help us, and everything will be done before you know it."

"Oh," Damon said quietly. He wrapped a little glass vase in newspaper and placed it carefully inside a box.

Jaden stood up and put a hand on Damon's shoulder. His grip was stronger than Damon expected. "We'll have all day tomorrow to hunt," Jaden said. "I'm going to sneak up to the attic and find that map."

Jaden ran off before Damon could respond.

Damon stayed in the room, wrapping and packing. Fifteen minutes later, Jaden returned. He was breathing heavily and his wicked grin was bigger than ever. "I found it!" he said.

"What?" Damon said. He jumped to his feet. "I don't believe it. Did you find it in the trunk?"

Jaden nodded. He held up the folded and frayed piece of paper in front of Damon's face. "Give it to me," Damon said, reaching out his hand.

Just then, the sound of footsteps came from the hall. Jaden quickly hid the piece of paper in his pocket.

"Hey, you two," Damon's mom said.

"Great news," Martha said. "The work is going more quickly than we thought."

"Yep," Mom said. "We can start loading up the truck now. Then we can relax tonight. In the morning, we can go say goodbye to Grandpa and head home."

Damon glanced at Jaden. He was frowning.

"I'm going to call the moving truck company," Mom said. "You two keep working, and we'll be back soon to help you finish."

The moms headed back downstairs. Damon glanced at Jaden. His smile was back.

"I guess we'll never get the chance to look for that treasure," Damon said, shrugging. He stood up and grabbed the packing tape.

"You're scared, aren't you?" Jaden said. "Well, guess what — we are still going to find the treasure."

"When?" Damon asked. "You heard my mom. We won't be here tomorrow."

"We'll look tonight," Jaden said. "After we get the truck loaded, I'm gonna say we're going to go get pizza."

"What if our moms want to come?" Damon said.

"I heard them say they were looking forward to ordering Chinese," Jaden said.

"I guess you have it all planned out," Damon said.

"I sure do," Jaden said. "And don't try to get out of it. You're coming with me."

Chapter 5: In Memory

Jaden and Damon walked down First Avenue toward downtown Ravens Pass. It was already very dark. Loading the truck had taken longer than their moms had predicted.

By the time Jaden had convinced his mom to let them get pizza, the full moon was hanging high in the sky.

"According to the treasure map," Jaden said, "we should head to the corner of Main and First Street."

"That's the busiest intersection in Ravens Pass," Damon said. "I really doubt there's a treasure there. Besides, I'm hungry. I want pizza."

Jaden rolled his eyes. "Obviously it's just the first step, dork," he said. "And don't worry, once we find the treasure, you can buy all the pizza you want."

Soon, they reached the corner of First and Main. Jaden stopped. "Here we are," he said.

"I'm not blind," Damon said. "Now what?"

Jaden looked at the map and scratched his head. He still hadn't even let Damon look at it. Some Ravens Pass residents shuffled past. They all seemed nervous and in a real hurry.

"You kids better get inside," a woman said as she passed. Her face was pale, and her eyes were deep. She looked tired, like she hadn't slept or smiled or laughed in years.

She squinted at Damon. "You look familiar," she said.

Damon shrugged. "I don't even live in this town," he said. "We're from Lakeville."

"Hmm," the woman said. "Well, the streets of Ravens Pass are no place for children, especially after dark." Then she stomped off.

"What is she talking about?" Jaden said with a laugh. "I guess your grandpa isn't the only one in Ravens Pass who's a little crazy, huh?"

Damon gave Jaden an angry look, but he didn't notice. He pointed at the map.

"There should be a clue nearby," Jaden said. "It says, 'Find the metal plaque near the smoking stack.'"

Damon looked around. "I don't see any smokestack," he said. "But I do see the pizza place."

"We'll eat later," Jaden said. He looked around.

"Jaden, can you hurry up?" Damon asked. "I'm starving, and it's getting cold."

"You're such a baby," Jaden said. "And don't act like you're not scared anymore. It's pretty obvious."

Jaden glanced up at the awning over their head. Then he smiled. "I found it," he said.

Damon looked up. "Old Plant Café" was written on the awning.

"I don't get it," he said. "Where's the smoking stack?"

"This is it," Jaden said. "Obviously this building used to be a factory."

Damon stared him. "'Plant' is another word for 'Factory,'" Jaden said. "Duh."

"So where do we go now?" Damon asked.

Jaden walked slowly along the wall of the café, looking at the sidewalk and at the red bricks of the building. "Here," he finally said. "A plaque."

Damon squinted at the square of metal. "I can't read it," he said. "The lettering is all faded."

Jaden pulled out his cell phone. He pushed a button so the light would come on. "This plaque is in memory of Esther Smith," he read aloud.

Damon frowned. "So what does it mean?" he asked.

Jaden frowned. He glanced at the plaque, and then at the map, and then back at the plaque. Then his sly, familiar grin appeared.

Jaden leaned in close to Damon. "Our next stop," he whispered, "is the graveyard."

— Chapter 6: Ravens Pass Cemetery —

"This is where I draw the line," Damon said. "I am not going to the cemetery."

He was hurrying next to Jaden, who was smirking as he walked with confidence along Main Street toward the old cemetery at the other end of town.

"You're just scared," Jaden said.

"Have you ever been to the Ravens Pass Cemetery?" Damon asked. "I have, when my grandma died. It's creepy!"

Jaden laughed. 'Nothing can hurt you in a cemetery, you scaredy-cat," he said. "Except . . . maybe . . ."

He turned and suddenly grabbed Damon by the shoulders. "ME!" he yelled.

Damon pushed his arms away. "Get off me!" he shouted.

Jaden burst out laughing. Damon glared at him. "That wasn't funny," Damon said.

"Yes it was," Jaden said. Then he started walking again. "If you don't want to find that treasure, then just run back home to your mommy."

Damon gritted his teeth. Then he hurried to catch up.

* * *

The big, iron gates of the cemetery were wide open.

Inside, a few stray cats slinked around the gate. There were some newer headstones near the entrance, but most of the gravestones were cracked. Several creepy statues cast long, eerie shadows in the moonlight.

"Wow, you weren't kidding," Jaden said. "This is one creepy cemetery."

"I told you," Damon said.

Jaden smiled. "Just my kind of place," he said, grabbing Damon's shirt and pulling him in.

"What are we looking for?" Damon asked.

Jaden weaved between tombstones and ducked under tree limbs. "A grave," he said.

"Here's one," Damon said, pointing at a cracked gravestone. "There's another. Oh look, and another." He stopped pointing. "Can we leave now?"

"You're hilarious," Jaden said, rolling his eyes. "We're looking for the grave of Esther Smith — the name on that plaque we found."

They moved slowly as they got deeper into the cemetery. The trees became uglier. The ivy grew wild along the crumbling brick walls. The tombstones were broken and chipped. Damon could barely read the names on some of them.

"We'll never find it," Damon said. "This is hopeless." Jaden didn't answer.

As they stepped over a fallen and cracked gravestone, something moved slowly in the shadows.

"What was that?" Damon whispered, bumping into Jaden.

Jaden twisted his head and stared for a long moment. Nothing moved except for tree branches that swayed in the wind.

Jaden started walking again. With his first step, he snapped a twig.

"Naughty children!" a voice cried out.

A figure darted out from the shadows and grabbed Jaden and Damon by their shoulders.

─ Chapter 7: Final Warning ─

"Get away from me!" Jaden screamed. He twisted and strained, but the woman held tight.

"Stop struggling," the woman said. She was shorter than Damon or Jaden. She wore a black cloak with its hood up over her head. The shadow it cast made seeing her face difficult.

Damon didn't dare try to pull away. "Who are you?" he asked.

The woman laughed. It sounded like a crow cackling.

Finally Jaden stopped squirming. "Let us go," he said, "or I'll scream so loud the police will come and arrest you!"

"The Ravens Pass police department?" the woman said. She laughed. "They're a joke. Where were they seventy years ago when Aaron Moone disappeared?"

"Aaron?" Damon repeated. "That must have been my grandpa's friend."

The woman peered at Damon. Then she threw back her hood. She was older than Damon would have guessed possible.

"I know your face," she said. "But it's not possible, it can't be you. You're too young!"

"I've never seen you before in my life," Damon said.

Jaden looked at the woman, then back at Damon. "She must think you're your grandpa," he said.

The woman nodded. "Yes, the grandson," she said. "That's why you little brats are here tonight, isn't it? You seek the treasure, just like that night seventy years ago."

"You know about the treasure?" Jaden asked.

The old lady gave Jaden a cockeyed glance. "You should not be here at night," she said. "Do not go to Esther Smith's grave. It will only bring death."

Jaden didn't speak for a moment. He just stared into the old woman's eyes. Damon saw that Jaden's face was stern and hard. His jaw was set. His eyes were narrow.

For an instant, Damon thought that Jaden was the creepy one — not the old lady.

Finally Jaden spoke. His voice was surprisingly calm. "You won't hurt us?" he asked.

The woman smirked. "You don't need to worry about me," she said. "There is great evil here among these graves."

"Well, we're not leaving," Jaden said. "So you might as well tell us where Esther Smith's grave is."

The woman shook her head sadly. She slowly raised a crooked finger and pointed at a crooked gravestone in a clearing not too far away.

Without another word, Jaden rushed toward the clearing.

Damon glanced at the strange woman and then chased after Jaden.

"Wait for me!" Damon cried.

"Please!" the woman called out. "If you must go inside Esther Smith's grave, don't take the other one with you!"

Jaden and Damon ran faster.

- Chapter 8: The Grave -

Jaden stopped running a few feet away from the gravestone. Damon bumped right into him. "Watch it!" he said, panting. "Did that crazy lady follow us?"

Damon turned to look back. No one was there. "I think she's gone," Damon said.

"Good," Jaden said. He pushed a button on his phone and shined the light on the gravestone. "Esther Smith" was etched into the top of the stone. "Bingo!" Jaden said.

Jaden lowered the light toward the ground. There was a big slab of marble over the burial plot. "That's weird," he said. "Usually graves are covered with grass."

They both kneeled in front of the marble slab. "What now?" Damon asked.

Jaden shrugged. "No idea," he said, tracing his fingers along the edge of the marble slab.

Damon glanced around nervously. "You should check the map for the next clue," he said.

Jaden pulled out the map. He read aloud, "Push the stone toward the moon and descend below into the gloom."

Jaden's eyes lit up. "This grave must be an entrance!" he said. He walked toward the gravestone. "Come help me push."

"Are you crazy?!" Damon said. "This is somebody's grave!"

"I don't think Esther will mind," Jaden said. "She's dead, remember?" Jaden pointed at the dates written on the stone. "Yep, she's dead all right — and has been for almost two hundred years."

Damon crossed his arms. "Nobody in their right mind would do this," he said.

"Your grandpa did," Jaden said. "Sixty years ago — maybe sixty years ago this very night — your grandpa and Aaron opened this coffin."

"You don't know that!" Damon said. "Maybe they never made it this far."

"You know they did," Jaden said. He walked slowly toward Damon. "You're just scared."

"So what if I am?" Damon said. "You're creepy! This whole thing is creepy! And I don't believe there is a treasure!"

Jaden clenched his jaw. He turned, put his hands on the gravestone, and pushed. Jaden grunted and struggled. Nothing happened. "What's going on?" Jaden asked. "It's not moving!"

Damon glanced skyward. "The map said to push the stone away from the moon," he said. "You're pushing the wrong way."

"Right," Jaden said. He walked to the other side of the stone and pushed his shoulder into it. Suddenly, the stone slid off its base and dropped to the ground with a great crash, shattering into pieces against the ground.

"You broke it!" Damon said, horrified.

Jaden shrugged. "So what?" he said.

Jaden looked down at the slab. "It's not moving," he said. "Shouldn't it be opening, or something?"

At that exact moment, a deep rumbling came from underground. Suddenly, the marble slab started to move. Jaden stepped back. "It's working!" he cried.

Inch by inch, the slab slid back. The bigger the opening became, the louder the rumbling sound was. Damon and Jaden pressed their hands to their ears. Then the sound stopped. The grave was open.

Jaden peered over the edge. He shrugged. "The grave is empty," he said. "It's fake."

Damon went over to see. It was the top of a staircase, not a grave at all. The steps led into the darkness below. "Man, this is too creepy," he said.

"I guess you're too afraid to come along then, huh?" Jaden said. Then he climbed in and started down the narrow, dark staircase.

Damon glanced around nervously. Then he followed Jaden inside.

— Chapter 9: Death —

Damon lost count of how many steps they'd taken. "We must be a hundred feet underground," he whispered to Jaden. Jaden didn't respond.

Moments later, the steps ended in a big, empty chamber. Jaden covered his mouth and nose with the top of his shirt. "Ugh," he said. "It stinks like your grandpa's place down here."

Damon came down the last steps and stood behind Jaden. "It does, doesn't it?" he said. But he didn't cover his nose. He just smiled.

Jaden turned and faced him. "What are you so happy about?" he asked. He spun and waved at the empty room. "There's nothing here. No treasure. Nothing."

"Not nothing," Damon said, smiling. "We're here now."

"Since when did you get a sense of humor?" Jaden asked, rolling his eyes. He pulled his shirt tighter to his face. "What is that horrible smell?"

"It's the smell of death," Damon said. He walked across the hard floor toward him. "And success."

Jaden took a step back, toward the steps. "What are you talking about?" he asked.

From the shadows, a figure stepped forward. "Who's there?!" Jaden cried out.

"You've done well, Damon," the man said.

Jaden shot a glance at Damon. "What is your grandpa doing here?!" he asked.

Jaden shined his cell phone's light in Damon's face. His features had changed. His ears seemed longer, and his teeth looked sharper. His mouth seemed bigger, too. Or maybe he was just smiling.

"You, Jaden, will be our next sacrifice," Damon said. "Grandpa is getting old again. It's time for him to feed."

Jaden screamed.

"Ah, that wonderful sound," Grandpa said. His voice sounded like gravel. "It reminds me of our last victim."

"Wha-what?" Jaden stammered.

"Isn't it obvious?" Grandpa asked.

Damon grinned. His smile seemed monstrous now. "That other boy in the picture you had," Damon said. "He was our last victim. He kept us the same ages for the last 70 years."

Grandpa chuckled. His voice was distorted and gruff. "And now," he said, "you will help us live another 70 years."

"I changed my mind, I don't want the treasure," Jaden whimpered. "I just want to go home."

Damon laughed. "There is no treasure," he said. A strange, purple glow surrounded him. "And you can't leave — not after all the trouble we went through to get you here."

Jaden backed up until he bumped into the wall. Damon and his grandpa crept toward Jaden, their mouths were open wide.

Case number: 232328

Date reported: September 17

Crime scene: Ravens Pass Cemetery

Local police: None

Victims: Jaden Kane, age 14

Civilian witnesses: None

Disturbance: Jaden Kane filed a report with police concerning a narrow escape from what he called "demons"

Suspects: Damon Germaine, true age unknown; his grandfather, David Germaine, true age unknown

Evidence: Jaden Kane's statement. Additionally, birth certificates for Damon Germaine and his grandfather, David, indicated they were both born over 200 years ago. Neither have been seen since the incident in Ravens Pass.

CASE NOTES:

IT'S MOST LIKELY THAT THE "DEMONS" JADEN KANE
CAME ACROSS WERE ACTUALLY WENDIGOS, A SPECIES OF
SHAPESHIFTERS FIRST SEEN BY NATIVE AMERICAN TRIBES
SEVERAL CENTURIES AGO. THE SPECIES HAS BEEN KNOWN
TO CONSUME THE BODIES OF THE LIVING IN ORDER TO
INCREASE ITS OWN LIFE SPAN. I DECIDED TO INVESTIGATE.

WHEN I ARRIVED AT RAVENS PASS CEMETERY, I FOUND
THE GRAVE THAT JADEN HAD MENTIONED. DOWN A
LONG FLIGHT OF STAIRS, I FOUND THE AREA WHERE
THE ATTEMPTED ASSAULT HAD OCCURRED. I TRACED MY
FINGERS ALONG THE EDGES OF THE CRYPT. IN THE BACK,
I FOUND A HIDDEN SWITCH AND PRESSED IT. IMMEDIATELY,
A GRANITE WALL SLID OPEN, REVEALING A HIDDEN
COMPARTMENT.

INSIDE, I FOUND THE TWO WENDIGOS. THEY BOTH
APPEARED TO BE OVER 200 YEARS OLD. IT SEEMS
THEY HAD HIDDEN THERE AFTER JADEN ESCAPED.
UNFORTUNATELY, BOTH OF THEM WERE DEAD. I HAVE TO
ASSUME, SINCE THEY WERE UNABLE TO FEED ON JADEN
AND PROLONG THEIR LIVES, TIME RAN OUT AND THEIR
BODIES AGED AT AN ACCELERATED RATE.

THEY WON'T BE EATING ANYONE AGAIN.

DEAR READER,

THEY ASKED ME TO WRITE ABOUT MYSELF. THE FIRST
THING YOU NEED TO KNOW IS THAT JASON STRANGE IS
NOT MY REAL NAME. IT'S A NAME I'VE TAKEN TO HIDE MY
TRUE IDENTITY AND PROTECT THE PEOPLE I CARE ABOUT.
YOU WOULDN'T BELIEVE THE THINGS I'VE SEEN, WHAT I'VE
WITNESSED. IF PEOPLE KNEW I WAS TELLING THESE STORIES,
SHARING THEM WITH THE WORLD, THEY'D TRY TO GET ME TO
STOP. BUT THESE STORIES NEED TO BE TOLD, AND I'M THE
ONLY ONE WHO CAN TELL THEM.

I CAN'T TELL YOU MANY DETAILS ABOUT MY LIFE. I CAN TELL
YOU I WAS BORN IN A SMALL TOWN AND LIVE IN ONE STILL. I
CAN TELL YOU I WAS A POLICE DETECTIVE HERE FOR TWENTY-
FIVE YEARS BEFORE I RETIRED. I CAN TELL YOU I'M STILL
OUT THERE EVERY DAY AND THAT CRAZY THINGS ARE STILL
HAPPENING.

I'LL LEAVE YOU WITH ONE QUESTION—IS ANY OF THIS TRUE?

JASON STRANGE
RAVENS PASS

Glossary

antique (an-TEEK)—a very old object

eerie (EER-ee)—strange, frightening, or unsettling

familiar (fuh-MIL-yur)—well-known or recognizable

hunchback (HUHNCH-bak)—a humped back

plaque (PLAK)—a plate with words inscribed on it that is usually placed on a wall in a public place

plot (PLOT)—to make a secret plan, or a small area of land, like a grave

recognize (REK-uhg-nize)—to see someone and know who they are

reputation (rep-yuh-TAY-shuhn)—what other people think of you

sacrifice (SAK-ruh-fisse)—the offering of someone or something in order to earn favor or fortune

scowled (SKOULD)—made an angry frown

shattered (SHAT-urd)—broke into tiny pieces

wicked (WIK-id)—evil or cruel

DISCUSSION QUESTIONS

1. Were you surprised by the ending of this book? Why or why not?

2. Jaden bosses Damon around until the end of this book. Have you had to deal with any bullies? Talk about bullies.

3. What was the scariest part of this book? Why?

WRITING PROMPTS

1. If you could live forever, what would you do with your life? Write about being an immortal.

2. Damon and his grandpa trick Jaden. Have you ever been tricked? What happened? Write about it.

3. This is a horror story about two monsters. Write your own horror story starring a monster you created.

Weird THINGS happen in RAVENS PASS.

JASON STRANGE

writes about them.

JASON STRANGE

BASEMENT OF THE UNDEAD

JASON STRANGE

Zombie Winter

JASON STRANGE

FULL MOON HORROR

JASON STRANGE

STRAYS

JASON STRANGE

THE DEMON CARD

JASON STRANGE

23 CROW'S PERCH

for more

monsters
GHOSTS
secrets

JASON STRANGE

creatures

visit us at www.capstonepub.com